MR DOG

AND THE RABBIT HABIT

First published in Great Britain by
HarperCollins *Children's Books* in 2019
HarperCollins *Children's Books* is a division of HarperCollins*Publishers* Ltd,
HarperCollins Publishers
1 London Bridge Street
London SE1 9GF

The HarperCollins website address is
www.harpercollins.co.uk
1

ISBN 978–0–00–830636–6

Ben Fogle and Nikolas Ilic assert the moral right to be identified
as the author and illustrator of the work respectively.
A CIP catalogue record for this title is available from the British Library.

Printed and bound in England by CPI Group (UK) Ltd, Croydon, CR0 4YY

MR DOG

AND THE RABBIT HABIT

BEN FOGLE

with Steve Cole

HarperCollins *Children's Books*

Mother Rabbit's burrow

Water scarecrow

Big New Fence

Rabbit-trap

About the Author

BEN FOGLE is a broadcaster and seasoned adventurer. A modern-day nomad and journeyman, he has travelled to more than a hundred countries and accomplished amazing feats, from swimming with crocodiles to rowing three thousand miles across the Atlantic Ocean; from crossing Antarctica on foot to surviving a year as a castaway on a remote Hebridean island. Most recently, Ben climbed Mount Everest. Oh, and he LOVES dogs.

To Ludo and Iona.
A life of love and respect for all
animals great and small.

Chapter One

MR DOG AND MOTHER RABBIT

The rabbit was running as fast as she could. The dog was gaining on her. Her fluffy white tail bobbed about as she darted left and right, trying to give him the slip. But the dog was too fast.

The rabbit rolled over on to her back as a long

furry snout loomed above her . . .

'Tag! You're it!' The dog nudged the bunny's

belly with his nose and snorted. 'Now it's your

turn to catch me – if you can!'

'Wait!' snuffled the rabbit. 'I'm all puffed out.'

'Very well. I *shall* wait.' The dog sat down for three seconds, then jumped straight up again, panting. 'There! Ready to play now?'

The rabbit thumped a hind leg in excitement. Most dogs she'd met were scary and chased you because they wanted to get you. This dog was different.

He was a scruffy, scraggy mutt, his coat black except for his white nose and front paws. In place of a collar he had a red and white hanky tied round his neck. His long tail swished all about, busy as a broom, and his shaggy eyebrows were full of expression.

11

'What's your name?' asked the curious rabbit.

'Mr Dog,' the dog replied. 'What's yours?'

'Mother Rabbit.' She paused, whiskers twitching. 'If you don't mind me saying so, Mr Dog is a funny name.'

'No, no, no. Figgy-Jig is a funny name.' Mr Dog danced a small jig on his hind legs. 'Bafflehonk, Wiggy and Dumpy-Drawers are all funny names. But Mr Dog is . . . elegant.' He bowed his head. 'Rather like myself!'

'Did your owners name you Mr Dog?'

'Owners?' Mr Dog's eyes widened. 'I don't have owners. I've had a few pet humans, if that's what you mean. But I prefer the travelling life.

Right now I'm staying in a garden.' He licked his nose. 'Perfectly nice woman who lives in the house, but she will insist on throwing away perfectly good balls, however many times I take them back.'

'Well, I've never gone further than this field,' Mother Rabbit admitted. 'I was born here, and so were my own bunnies. They're sleeping in their nest right now.' She got up and stretched. 'I have to wait until dusk before I go back to feed them. I'd hate to lead something hungry and horrible there.'

'Quite right.' Mr Dog snuffled at her. 'So . . . another game of tag, then?'

'No, thank you.' Mother Rabbit wrinkled her nose. 'I need my strength to mind my little ones. I'm hungry – and my nose smells fresh carrots!'

'Carrots?' Mr Dog looked around. There was only grass in the big field for as far as he could see . . . grass that was surrounded by two big green hedges and one solid wooden fence. Beyond the fence, Mr Dog could just see the tops of some tents and caravans. 'There aren't any carrots growing around here, Mother Rabbit. But maybe there are humans eating carrots behind that fence?'

'The Big New Fence, you mean? Goodness knows what happens behind there.' Mother

Rabbit's ears waggled and she shook her head.

'Now, if you'll excuse me, Mr Dog, my nose is *extra*-clever when it comes to carrots. I can smell them . . . this way!' And off she hopped towards the nearest hedgerow.

Mr Dog watched her go. 'Ah well,' he said. 'There are loads of other rabbits here. Maybe one or two of them would like to play?'

But the next moment his ragged ears pricked straight up at a squeak of dismay from the hedgerow. It was Mother Rabbit, he realised, and ran off to investigate.

15

Soon he saw what Mother Rabbit had not –
there was a trap hidden in the long grass. As
she'd run inside it to get the carrot she must have
knocked a stick holding the trap door up. Now it
had snapped down, and she was caught inside.

'Help!' Mother Rabbit was hopping about
anxiously. 'I can't get out! What is this thing?'

'I'm afraid it's a rabbit trap.' Mr Dog pushed
his muzzle up against the catch on the door,
but it was on a steel spring and wouldn't open.
He batted at it with both paws, but soon his tail
drooped. 'It's no good. I can't get you out!'

'Oh no.' Mother Rabbit looked at Mr Dog
with wide eyes.

'So many bunnies have gone missing from these fields ever since the Big New Fence went up. I thought they'd just hopped away. They must have been caught, like me!'

'But why?' Mr Dog felt sad. 'What harm can rabbits be doing running around and burrowing in a field?'

'I just don't know.' Mother Rabbit shook her head. 'Oh, Mr Dog! What about my poor little bunnies, asleep in our burrow? They're only two weeks old! What will become of them if I never come back?'

Mr Dog knew the answer, and it wasn't good. 'You *will* come back. There must be a way to open this rotten thing . . . He closed his jaws round the wire of the trap door and rattled it. 'Come on, come on . . .'

'*Oi, dog! Get away from that rabbit!*'

Busily trying to force open the cage, Mr Dog

hadn't noticed a young man with dark hair and

muddy clothes close by. 'Where did you come

from?' he woofed in surprise.

Of course, the man didn't understand him. He

just picked up the trap with Mother Rabbit in it

and turned away.

'Dear me, what shocking manners

you have.' Mr Dog grabbed

the leg of the man's jeans

in his jaws and

tugged very hard.

'Mmm, but what

tasty trousers!'

'Hey, get off – WHOA!' The man tried to pull away but overbalanced and fell to his knees. He put down the trap. 'Silly dog!'

'Close, but my first name is *Mister*, thank you very much!' Mr Dog scrabbled again at the door to the trap, trying desperately to pull it open.

'Mr Dog!' Mother Rabbit spoke quickly. 'You can't help me, but please help my little ones. If you find another mother rabbit with a litter like me, perhaps she'll take them in? Follow the Big New Fence towards the road,' she went on. 'You'll find our burrow there.'

'I promise I'll help.' Mr Dog looked into her dark and frightened eyes. 'I'll get you out. You'll see.'

By now the man had got back to his feet and was glaring down at Mr Dog. He reached for the spotted hanky round Mr Dog's neck. 'Aha, no collar on you – just a neckerchief – which means that you probably don't have an owner. And if you don't have an owner, then it's the dog pound for you . . .'

The man's fingers seized hold of the fabric. Now Mr Dog was trapped too!

Chapter Two

WHITE RABBIT

'**U**nhand me, sir!'
Mr Dog barked.

Desperately he turned in a tight circle to break the man's grip on his neckerchief and then sprang backwards. The man reached out to try to catch him, but Mr Dog ran away as fast as a racehorse – if not slightly faster.

'I'll be back!' Mr Dog panted. 'Keep your furry chin up, Mother Rabbit!' He looked over his shoulder and was pleased to see that the man wasn't following him. Even so, Mr Dog kept running. *I can't take any chances,* he thought. *If anything happens to me now, I'll never reach those poor bunnies . . .*

Suddenly, something in the ground sprayed jets of cold water all round, splashing him all over. 'UGH!' Mr Dog was soaked in a second, and quickly changed direction, running for shelter in the nearest long grass. 'Whatever was that?'

As he looked back, Mr Dog saw that the powerful spray had sent some rabbits running away too. He realised he'd seen something like it before in a garden he'd stayed in. 'Must be a sprinkler that goes off to scare any animal that comes near.' He licked his nose, still panting for breath. 'But who would leave such a thing out here?'

Peering through the tall grass, Mr Dog saw a long hosepipe snaking from the water sprinkler. It stretched all the way to the Big New

Fence. Across the field, the man from before was walking towards the fence with the trap containing Mother Rabbit in his arms.

A door swung open in the fence and both man and trap went through it.

'Most mysterious,' mused Mr Dog. 'Whoever's behind the Big New Fence, it seems they really don't like rabbits. But why?' He got to his feet.

'Well, I'll just have to find out. I wonder if there's
a sneaky hound-shaped back way in . . .?'

But as Mr Dog began trotting across the field
towards the fence – being careful to avoid the water
sprinkler – he spotted something that surprised
him. (And Mr Dog was surprisingly hard to surprise.)

Sitting by the corner of the fence in the field
was a rabbit who looked very different from all
the other rabbits he'd ever met in the wild. It was
bigger, white and fluffy, with
enormous lop ears.

'That's an angora rabbit.
A *pet* rabbit!'

Confused, Mr Dog scratched the side of his head with his back leg. Whatever was a pet rabbit doing out here? *Perhaps*, he thought, *it belongs to someone who lives behind the Big New Fence?* He jumped up in sudden excitement. 'If the rabbit's found a way out, perhaps I can use it as a way in – and reach Mother Rabbit!' Mr Dog stood up on his back legs and waved his paws.'Hey, you – white and fluffy! Over here!'

At the sight of Mr Dog, the big white rabbit turned and bolted away.

'Wait!' Mr Dog barked. 'I only want to talk to you!'

He ran after the big rabbit, but by the time he'd reached the corner of the fence it had vanished from sight. Mr Dog knew that there was a rabbit warren full of tunnels in the long grass. Perhaps one of the holes led under the fence to whatever was on the other side?

Or perhaps it might go to Mother Rabbit's little bunnies! Mr Dog remembered that she didn't want to lead predators to her tiny ones, and so wouldn't return until dusk.

'I shall stand a stick in front of every rabbit hole,' Mr Dog decided, 'then I'll come back at sunset. If the stick's been knocked aside, I'll know a mummy bunny has called by. If the stick is still standing there, it means no one's been in or out. That hole might lead to Mother Rabbit's home . . . and have hungry little ones inside!'

Mr Dog fetched several sticks and placed one outside every rabbit hole he could see. Then he left the field and went back to his adopted garden.

When he returned at sundown with a belly full of food – a fitting reward, he felt, for all the balls he'd had to chase and fetch – Mr Dog surveyed the burrows in the gathering dark. All of the sticks he'd placed at the entrance to the rabbit holes had been pushed aside – except one.

Mr Dog felt a pang of sadness at the thought of what he had to tell the little bunnies within. He crossed over to that particular hole in the grass and pushed his head inside. 'Hello?' he called. 'Anyone home?' His ears were folded down over his head, but still Mr Dog could hear little whimpers and shivering bodies. He blinked, his keen eyes growing accustomed to the dark. 'I'm terribly sorry, but your mother has had to, er, go away for a bit. I'm here to help you find a new place to stay.'

'Mama's gone?' came a quiet high-pitched voice.

'Mama's left us?' came another.

'She didn't *want* to go.' Mr Dog's heart felt as heavy as an elephant. 'Don't worry. I'm going to do my very best to get you all back together again.'

A third voice came out of the darkness. 'But why would a dog help a rabbit?' It sounded deeper than the first two. 'Dogs hunt rabbits. Dogs *eat* rabbits.'

'Well, *Mr* Dog doesn't!' growled Mr Dog indignantly.

'Mr Dog? Why should we trust you?'

'Because D-O-G is the first part of DO GOOD – and that's this mutt's motto!' He grinned. 'I'm going to pull my head out of your home now, and wait for you all to come and join me.'

Mr Dog carefully wriggled free and checked to make sure that there weren't any dangers about. There were lots of other rabbits in the fields, some watching him warily, so he gave them his cheeriest smile. He wondered if any would be willing to make space for a couple more bunnies in their burrows.

He waited for several minutes and eventually a very small rabbit, barely bigger than a tennis ball, crawled cautiously from the burrow. She was brown with tiny ears and big black eyes. Behind her came another small brown bunny, a boy, smaller than his sister and sleepier too. A second girl soon followed, the smallest of all. The siblings sat side by side, looking up at Mr Dog.

'Are you sure you won't eat us?' whimpered the tiny girl bunny.

'Certain,' said Mr Dog.

The bunny's big sister turned back to the burrow. 'It's all right,' she squeaked, 'we haven't been eaten. You can come out too.'

Another rabbit emerged from behind the brother and sister. Only this one was easily twice their size with white fur, floppy ears and a pink twitching nose.

Mr Dog's eyes grew wider. 'That angora rabbit I saw – it's *you*!'

Chapter Three

THE STORY OF SOCKS

'Angora? What are you talking about?' The white rabbit shook his head. 'I'm just a regular wild rabbit like, er, my brother and sisters here.'

Mr Dog's shaggy eyebrows shot up into the air. 'Your brother and sisters?' he spluttered.

'You can't fool me!'

'It's true, mister.' The littlest girl bunny wiggled her tail. 'He's been in our burrow for as long as I can remember.'

'And how long is that?'

'Since yesterday,' squeaked the little boy bunny.

'Day *before* yesterday,' said the elder girl bunny proudly.

The white rabbit whimpered. 'See? Proof positive that we all have the same mum. Now, where is she? We little babies can't look after ourselves, you know.'

'Babies?' Mr Dog boggled. This rabbit was

big – at least two years old. What was he up to?

'Do you think we might have a talk in private, Mr . . . ?'

'Socks,' squeaked the Angora. 'My name is Socks. All right, then, Mr Dog. A private word. But just quickly.' He turned to the baby bunnies. 'Hop back inside your burrow. I'll join you in a minute.'

'Okay, Socks.' The bunnies hopped inside.

Mr Dog lay down beside the Angora rabbit so that they were eye to eye. 'So, tell me, Socks,' he said. 'Why are you pretending that you belong with these wild rabbits?'

'But I do belong with them!' Socks began. 'I

know I look larger than them, but I'm just big boned—'

'Come off it, Socks!' Mr Dog shook his head sternly. 'Admit it. You're not a wild rabbit – you're a pet!'

'No, no, I . . .' His whiskers drooped and he sighed. 'Oh, all right, it's true. I am.' He looked up sadly at Mr Dog. 'What gave me away?'

Mr Dog cocked his head to one side, considering. 'Oooh, not much. Apart from just about everything. What are you up to? I thought perhaps you came from the other side of the Big New Fence.'

'Oh no,' Socks said quickly. 'I come from

a hutch inside a house with a nice garden. I'm not sure where it is. But my owners brought me out here a few days ago . . . and turned me loose.'

'What?' Mr Dog's ears stood up straight. 'How could they do such a thing? A pet can't survive in the wild!'

'I'm sure they didn't mean to leave me.' Socks washed his whiskers. 'I think they were probably just letting me have a bit of a run around. But then they just got back into the car and . . . well, I suppose they forgot that they hadn't picked me up. They drove away without me.' He smiled bravely. 'They'll be back, though! I watch the road each day waiting for their car. It was red, I think. Or green . . .'

Mr Dog looked sadly at the deflated rabbit. He knew that unwanted pet rabbits were sometimes released into the wild. The human owners thought they were doing a nice thing – but they weren't.

'Now I see why you're here,' said Mr Dog. 'Pet rabbits need looking after, so you're trying to fit in with Mother Rabbit's little ones.'

'I thought that she might look after me along with her real bunnies,' Socks admitted. 'She lost

three of her little ones when
a fox raided the warren. I
thought having me to look
after would make her feel
better. But now you say she's gone . . .?'

'Taken away in a cage by a muddy man,' Mr
Dog agreed. 'Socks, you have to understand:
even if she did look after you, young bunnies in
the wild only stay with their mothers for a few
weeks. You'd soon end up on your own again.'

'Yes, but by then my owners would have come
back for me,' Socks said, although he did look a
little uncertain. 'They wouldn't leave me out here
for ever. Would they?'

Mr Dog didn't reply. He had the saddest feeling that Socks's owners were never coming back.

Suddenly, a scent was carried to him on the air and his ears pricked up. Rabbits were scattering all about and in the distance he could see a torch bobbing. Then, through the twilight gloom, he saw the sleek frame of another dog running towards the warren. As it got closer Mr Dog could see it was a lurcher.

'It's a hunting dog, after rabbits!' Mr Dog batted Socks towards the burrow with his scruffy tail. 'Quick! Get out of sight. Baby bunnies have no scent but you do!'

42

'Eeek!' Quick as a flash, Socks shot back inside the rabbit hole. 'I hate the wild. I'm never coming out again!'

Mr Dog was already down on his haunches, moving in a commando crawl towards the cover of some bushes so he could keep an eye on what was going on, while staying out of sight. The lurcher was running at incredible speed – it had been trained to catch rabbits, and that's what it was out to do! With horror, Mr Dog saw that the hunting hound was headed for a bunch of bunnies who were oblivious to the danger.

What could he do?

Desperately, making all the noise he could

muster, Mr Dog burst from the bushes and ran for the rabbits himself, woofing at the top of his lungs. The rabbits jumped in the air and fled.

The lurcher arrived on the scene a moment later, panting for breath. 'You fool!' he snarled at Mr Dog. 'You scared them all away before I could even catch one!'

Mr Dog assumed an innocent air. 'My dear fellow, I'm so very sorry. I was trying to hunt those rabbits myself, but I'm afraid I'm not very good at it.

Not like you – you seem to be

a real expert.'

'Well, yes, I am, since you happen to mention

it.' The lurcher looked at him suspiciously. 'Why

are you here? Where's your owner?'

'Oh, somewhere about,' Mr Dog said

vaguely. 'He set me loose to catch a

rabbit but, well – I'm no lurcher,

am I? I nearly got one but it

ended up getting caught in a trap!

Then a man took it away through the

Big New Fence.'

'Yes, I'm sure,' said the lurcher. 'They've got dozens of rabbits caged up in there.'

'Why do you think that is?' Mr Dog asked him. 'What are they up to?'

'Digging, my owner says.' The lurcher looked back as his owner called to him. 'She'll be cross with me now. All the rabbits have scattered and I haven't caught a single one.'

'I can't say sorry enough,' said Mr Dog, hiding his smile. 'But I'm sure you'll be back.'

'Not for much longer,' the lurcher said. 'The people digging behind the fence are trying to control the rabbits with traps and scarers and clever hunting dogs like me, but it's not working.

My owner says they're going to deal with them permanently.'

'Permanently?' echoed Mr Dog. 'You mean for ever, for good, no turning back? Why, whatever could they be planning?'

But the lurcher had sprinted away at its owner's call, leaving Mr Dog alone – and feeling very, very worried.

Chapter Four

DIGGING DEEP

It proved to be a busy evening for Mr Dog.

The lurcher and his owner ended up

hanging around for hours, trying to catch rabbits

or simply chasing them into nets. Mr Dog had

to sneak about pulling the nets off or scaring the

bunnies away without being spotted.

At last, the lurcher and his owner gave up and went away . . . through the same door in the Big New Fence.

Exhausted, Mr Dog went back to the burrow.

Socks nervously pushed his head out. 'What happened back there?'

'The people behind that fence have *really* got it in for rabbits . . .' Mr Dog explained what he'd done and all he'd seen.

'So, the rabbits are going to be dealt with p-p-permanently?' Socks twitched his little pink nose in alarm. 'That's awful. What if my owners haven't come back to me by then?'

'And what about all the rabbits in these

fields?' Mr Dog lay down again, shaking his head.

'Somehow I've got to find Mother Rabbit, put

her back with her bunnies, and help all the other

rabbits too—'

'Including me?' Socks said hopefully.

Mr Dog looked at him and smiled. 'Yes, I'd

like to help you too, Socks.'

'Brilliant!' Socks hopped up and down. 'But

why would you help us? You're a free dog – you

could go anywhere you like.'

 'And leave animals in danger

without at least trying to

help them?' Mr Dog tutted.

'That's just not me. No, no,

that wouldn't do at all. What if I were the one in danger? I'd like to think other animals would help me if I were in trouble.' He looked pointedly at Socks. 'Animals like you – you'll help me, won't you?'

Socks looked nervous. 'Er . . . What are you going to do?'

'Isn't it obvious?' Mr Dog grinned. 'The answers – and the rabbits – lie behind the Big New Fence. Somehow we have to get inside!'

*

The young bunnies and Socks needed their sleep. Mr Dog lay outside their burrow like a guard dog until the dawn scattered its light on the world. The birds began to call and, like the other beasts, the rabbits began to busy themselves with grooming and feeding.

Mr Dog could tell that Mother Rabbit's bunnies were very hungry. They were too young to eat solid food – they needed milk. Mr Dog knew that if they went without it much longer they'd grow dehydrated and die.

'My tummy hurts,' said the older girl bunny.

'Mine hurts more,' said the boy.

'Mine hurts most,' squeaked their little sister.

'I had hoped to leave you bunnies behind in your burrow and bring your mother back to you,' said Mr Dog. 'But that might take too long – you need her milk now. You'll just have to come with us.'

'Come with you where, Mr Dog?' asked the boy, sleepy-eyed.

'Where?' Mr Dog struck a heroic pose. 'Why, behind the fence, of course!'

'Eeek!' Socks jumped in the air. 'That sounds scary!'

'I think you mean *exciting*, Socks.' Mr Dog gave him a stern look. 'Now, young bunnies, we're going on an adventure, and I may need to speak to you quickly. I can't be saying, "Hey, there, boy bunny!" or "Watch out there, girl bunny!" What are your names?'

'Mother hasn't named us yet.' The elder girl bunny wiggled her nose. 'Why don't you give us names, Mr Dog?'

Mr Dog considered. 'Well, in keeping with the footwear theme started by Socks, how about I call you Sneaker, your brother Shoe, and your little sister Flip-Flop?'

The bunnies laughed. 'Flip-Flop!' squeaked Flip-Flop.

'Sneaker!' said Shoe.

'Shoe!' said Sneaker.

'We had all better "shoo"!' Mr Dog stretched, shook his fur to straighten the hanky round his neck and then padded over to the huge fence. Going over it was not an option . . . but perhaps they could tunnel under it?

'Any good at burrowing, Socks?' Mr Dog began scuffing at the turf around the base of the fence. 'The quickest way to get in is to go right under here.'

'Before the people wake up?' Socks said, nodding. 'Good idea. People stay asleep for ages.'

'Right.' Mr Dog began digging with his front

paws, spraying dirt in all directions. 'We can have a good nose about and won't be noticed.'

Socks joined in the digging. Sneaker, Shoe and Flip-Flop tried too, but kept falling over clods of earth.

'Something's wrong.' Mr Dog peered down at the hole they were making. 'Our tunnel's not getting any deeper.'

'Something's blocking the way down there.' Socks jumped in and cooed. 'Oooh! It's like the front of my old hutch. Happy days . . .'

Mr Dog sighed. 'It's chicken wire.'

'I didn't know chickens made wire,' said Shoe.

'They don't. They make eggs. Anything else would be *eggs*-tremely silly.' Mr Dog nudged Socks out of the hole with his nose. 'The builders of this fence have obviously put chicken wire underground to stop you rabbits digging underneath it.'

'Sneaky devils.' Socks clambered up a small hillock and looked towards the distant road. 'Oh well. Let's give up and wait for my owners to arrive.'

'I think we'll be waiting a long time,' Mr Dog growled. 'Besides, I don't like giving up. Did Wellington give up? Did Lincoln? Did Churchill?'

'Who are they?' asked Sneaker.

'These three Labradors I met once. When they got a bone, they *never* gave it up. Most inspiring!' He gave an encouraging grin. 'Come on, let's go right the way round this fence, looking for a better way in. Perhaps they haven't laid chicken wire all the way around . . .'

The curious-looking group made their way

along the fence as the sun began its slow ascent into the sky. Mr Dog tried digging down at various points, but each time he came up against the same thing – more dreaded chicken wire.

'I'm still hungry,' said Flip-Flop.

'Me too,' said Shoe.

'Try grass,' said Socks, munching on a slender stem.

'No, don't!' Mr Dog barked. 'That could be bad for your tummies. Your mum's milk is super-nutritious; it gives you all you need to get by. I don't think you're ready to start eating grass yet.'

Sneaker gave a little sigh. 'How come you know so much about it, Mr Dog?'

59

'Well, a doctor makes people well – and the D-O-G in my name is short for *dog*-tor!' He licked his sore claw. 'Well, maybe. Come along. We must stay busy – that will help keep your minds off your tummies.'

'I thought my mind was in my head,' said Flip-Flop.

'What mind?' teased Shoe.

Socks nudged all three bunnies along. 'Come on, let's speed this up.'

Following the fence, they came to another sharp corner. As they turned it, a shadow fell over them and Socks gave a loud squeak of horror. It was the shadow of a hunting bird!

'Behind me, everyone!' cried Mr Dog, standing up on his back legs. Socks gasped, squashed, as the little rabbits bundled up around him.

Snarling, Mr Dog studied the sky. There was no hunting bird to be seen – and yet the shadow was still visible on the grass by the fence.

Then he saw that the shadow was being cast by a flat metal cut-out of a bird hanging from a wire wrapped round a wooden post in the ground.

'Phew!' Mr Dog dropped back to all fours and turned to his party of rabbits. 'It's all right. It's just a sort of scarecrow to scare you little furry foragers away.'

'People are mean,' said Sneaker sadly.

'So mean,' Flip-Flop agreed.

'And my tummy still hurts,' added Shoe.

'After the way you charged into me, so does mine!' said Socks.

'Hush now, children.' Mr Dog was eyeing the post. 'If the scarecrow has been placed here, perhaps the chicken wire hasn't? Let's find out.'

His front legs were aching by now, but Mr Dog dutifully dug once again in the wavering shadow of the make-believe bird of prey. 'Don't be scared of the scarecrow,' he panted as he worked. 'Remember, it can't hurt you.'

It wasn't long before Mr Dog struck wire netting again. Feeling cross, he moved a few metres along and tried digging again. Surely there had to be some part of the Big New Fence that was unprotected? The shadow of the hunting bird flitted around him in a circle, but he took no notice.

For at least three seconds.

That was when he realised he had moved well away from the scarecrow silhouette of the bird of prey. So how could it still be hanging over him?

With a gasp of horror Mr Dog looked up. The silhouette had been joined by a real hunting bird. A red kite was swooping down towards the bunnies, its deadly talons outstretched to snatch them up!

Chapter Five

UNDER THE FENCE

Even as Mr Dog opened his jaws to bark a warning, he knew it was too late. The red kite was a swift and powerful hunter. As it dropped from the sky to make a catch, its curved beak opened, ready to bite down on the baby bunnies.

But Socks had seen the danger already. His powerful hind legs propelled him forward and he knocked Shoe, Sneaker and Flip-Flop flying. The red kite caught only grass in its talons and rose up again into the sky.

Mr Dog barked, 'Quick! Hide in the hole!'

All four rabbits ducked into the dip in the ground and Mr Dog lay down over them, hiding them from view. The red kite circled once more, then tipped away, looking for easier prey elsewhere.

'That was close!' came Sneaker's muffled voice.

'Sneaker, you're sitting on my head,' snuffled Shoe.

'Who's sitting on mine?' sniffed Flip-Flop. 'I don't dare open my eyes!'

'I think I am,' said Socks. 'Sorry. I'm shaking all over.'

Mr Dog quickly got off and smiled down at Socks. 'Well, if you stop shaking, I'll shake your paw! You were very brave, Socks. You saved those bunnies' lives!'

'Did I?' Socks seemed in a daze as he climbed out. 'Well, I had to do something . . . We're family, aren't we?'

'Right!' Shoe hopped out of the hole with Flip-Flop and they both nudged up to him.

But Sneaker didn't follow. 'Hey, Socks,' she squeaked from somewhere in the hole, 'did you burrow further down?'

'I did,' Socks agreed. 'I didn't know what else to do.'

'But how could you? The wire was in the way . . . wasn't it?' Mr Dog padded closer to the hole and smiled. 'Well, well! Look what's happened! You've found the edge of the netting. There must be a gap before the next stretch of chicken wire starts – that's why the scarecrow's here.'

Shoe hopped about excitedly. 'So we can get under the fence?'

'We can find our mum?' asked Flip-Flop.

'Let's hope so,' Mr Dog agreed. 'Come on, everyone. Let's get burrowing!'

So quietly, bravely, all four animals dug, delved and burrowed through the mud as best they could. The rabbits went first, making a narrow tunnel beneath the Big New Fence. Then they sat back and caught their breath while Mr Dog took a turn, shovelling with his paws to widen it so that he could fit through too. He kicked up a shower of mud – mud and something else . . .

'Ow!' said Socks. 'Something just knocked me on the head!'

'Hey, what's that?' said Shoe.

'It's shiny!' said Sneaker.

Flip-Flop licked it. 'Ugh! It doesn't taste good.'

'Let me see.' Mr Dog turned and frowned at the sight of a small gold disc on the ground. 'That's a coin, isn't it? I wonder what that was doing buried in the mud?'

'I don't suppose it was doing much at all,' said Sneaker wisely.

'A human must've dropped it.' Socks sniffed at a clod of earth and it crumbled. 'Look, there are more here.'

Mr Dog examined the coins. They looked to be gold, and very, very old: they were quite wonky.

If we were humans, we could buy milk for the bunnies with these, thought Mr Dog. *But coins are useless for animals.*

'Is the tunnel nearly finished?' asked Sneaker softly.

'Won't be long now.' Mr Dog nibbled some mud from his fur. 'One last push, and we'll make it for sure. Here goes . . .!'

After digging and scrabbling and growling and pushing, Mr Dog finally broke through the ground, snout first.

He gulped down breaths as he looked all about.

He had emerged on the other side of the Big New Fence to discover . . . mud! Piles and piles of mud lay heaped all round the edges of what seemed to be the ruins of a very old courtyard – the craggy remains of drystone walls half buried in sandy soil. Several pits had been dug inside the crumbling walls, each marked out with lengths of string tied between tent pegs. Wooden racks held old cups and bowls, each carefully labelled. Beyond the mud and the stone ruins stood an old caravan connected to a squat black and green generator that was taking electricity to two large grey Portakabins, a couple of tents and an old snack van, its serving window closed.

'*This* is what the humans built their fence round?' said Socks, struggling through beside him. 'What a dump!'

Sneaker agreed. 'It's just full of dirt and stones and stuff.'

'There must be a point to this place.' Mr Dog sniffed the air. 'The humans wouldn't go to the trouble of building that fence and trying to deal with you rabbits if it wasn't important . . .'

'Well, no rabbit would come here unless they had to!' Socks declared. 'There's nothing to eat for a start!'

'But, thank goodness, there *is* something to drink!' Mr Dog had spied a small bowl of water on the ground beside the caravan. Perhaps it belonged to the lurcher? He trotted over with some relief. 'My mouth is as dry as a hamster's cheek pouch . . .' He lapped thirstily at the water. 'Ahhh, that's better.'

'*I disagree!*'

The voice, cold and supercilious, made Socks and the bunnies duck back into their hole.

Mr Dog froze. Who had discovered them?

Chapter Six

THE BLACK CAT

Mr Dog turned round quickly to find a black cat sauntering out from behind the wheel of the caravan. She was swishing her tail from side to side. Her green eyes glittered.

'What is that thing?' squeaked Shoe.

'It's a monster!' Sneaker squealed. 'Can it fly?'

'No,' said Socks, 'but your fur will if it catches

you. It's a cat. A big horrible cat!'

'My name is Kitty and this is my site.' Her

green eyes met Mr Dog's. 'Who are you?'

Now, Mr Dog didn't care much for cats, but he tried to treat them with respect, the same as all the animals he met. He'd known some dogs who loved to chase cats, and known several cats who loved to fight back with a serious scratch to the nose. Mr Dog had the feeling that Kitty fell very much into that group – and since he was rather fond of his nose he decided it was best to be friendly. 'Greetings, Kitty! My name's Mr Dog, and my rabbity friends are Socks, Shoe, Flip-Flop and Sneaker. So, this is your site, is it? Congratulations – and may I say that your water dish is definitely a *sight* for sore eyes!'

'You drank from my dish. Which means

you're a thief as well as an intruder.' Kitty looked past him and stared at the rabbits. 'The humans here would go mad if they saw you all running about. None of you should be here.' Her eyes glittered as she licked her lips. 'This place is a Site of Great Historical Importance, you know.'

'A what of who?' said Socks, baffled.

Kitty gave him a disdainful look. 'Have you never heard of *archaeology*?'

'Ark-ay-oll-oh-jee?' Flip-Flop struggled to get her tiny bunny lips around the big word. 'I've never heard of it. Any of you bunnies ever heard of it?'

'Nope,' squeaked Sneaker.

'We're only two weeks old,' Shoe explained, 'we've hardly heard of anything!'

'But I have!' Mr Dog yelped. 'Of course. What a silly dog I've been!'

'Keep your woofing down,' hissed Kitty. 'Or you'll wake my servants. Some of them live here on site.'

Mr Dog swung round to Socks and the bunnies, still peeping wide-eyed from the mouth of the tunnel. 'She doesn't really have servants. This place is what's known as a dig. The people in charge here are *archaeologists* – people who learn about ancient cultures by digging up the things they left behind. Buildings, tools, jewellery . . .'

'And old coins! That's why they were buried in the mud.' Socks's nose was twitching with excitement. 'So, people used to live here long ago?'

Kitty nodded. 'There was a fort here back in Roman times, so the ground is full of its ruins and old bits and bobs.'

'But rabbits don't care about stuff like that, do they?' Mr Dog reasoned. 'So why are your "servants" trying to get rid of them?'

'Because rabbits mess up the whole dig site!' Kitty glared at Socks, Shoe, Flip-Flop and Sneaker. 'My servants moan about your lot all the time. Rabbits dig deep into the soil, making their burrows and warrens. That undermines the foundations of the ruins so that they fall apart faster. The different layers of old stuff get jumbled up so it's harder to know just how things were left and who left them there . . .'

'So that's why they've been trying to keep rabbit numbers down.' Mr Dog gave Kitty what he hoped was his most appealing smile. 'I saw a rabbit being brought in here yesterday afternoon. Do you know where we can find her?'

'How dare you ask me to help you!' Kitty arched her back and hissed. Mr Dog stepped away and the rabbits squealed in harmony. 'You have a nerve, you scruffy mutt.'

'Scruffy?' Mr Dog scratched his ear with his back leg. 'I'll have you know my neckerchief is the height of fashion!'

'You break into MY site, drink from MY water dish, listen to MY explanations without even a thank-you, and THEN you expect favours!' Kitty smiled and shook her head. 'If you want to stay here a minute longer, it's going to cost you . . . one bunny.'

Mr Dog flattened his ears to his head, horrified. 'Excuse me?'

Kitty's green eyes were sparkling. 'Give me

one of the bunnies to play with – just one – and
perhaps I'll tell you more.'

'I'll do it!' Shoe jumped up and down. 'I love
playing!'

'No,' said Socks quickly. 'This is one game you
would never win.'

Mr Dog decided it was time to bare his teeth a
little. 'What if we *don't* give you a bunny?'

Kitty hissed again and slashed at Mr Dog
with her sharp claws. A red strip of fabric was
torn clear from his
neckerchief
collar.

Mr Dog stared down at it and gulped.

'Just do as I say, or you'll be sorry. I'll howl and yowl and wake everyone up.' Kitty sat beside her water dish and grinned nastily at the rabbits. 'By the way, if you try to run, remember that I'm faster than you. I'll quickly catch up, and maybe then I'll eat two rabbits . . . or even THREE.'

Mr Dog looked at Socks, Sneaker, Flip-Flop and Shoe, who had started to shiver.

'I'm afraid we have no choice,' he said softly.

'Which of you wants to come and . . . play with Kitty the cat, here, hmm?'

'None of us!' Socks jumped up, appalled. 'You can't let this fleabag get her way.'

'On the contrary,' said Mr Dog. 'I'm going to give her what she deserves.' He winked carefully at the rabbits, then turned to Flip-Flop. 'Hop over here, little one. Please?'

'Okay, Mr Dog,' said Flip-Flop, looking up at him with worried black eyes.

'It's all right.' Mr Dog lifted her gently in his jaws. 'Just remember – when I drop you, close your eyes.' He turned and crossed back towards

Kitty. 'Here,' he growled through a mouthful of fur, 'will this one do?'

'Yes!' Kitty declared, licking her lips as she laughed. 'It's skinny and small, but I'll still have some fun with it!'

'Don't forget, though, Kitty,' Mr Dog added, 'you should always wash your paws before a meal.' ('Get ready, Flip-Flop!' he whispered.) 'Here, let us help you out . . .'

And suddenly, with a flick of his neck, Mr Dog dropped Flip-Flop into the cat's water dish.

SPLOOOSH!

The little rabbit made a big impact, sending

cold water flying all over Kitty! Surprised, the

cat jumped backwards – straight into the rack

of old relics. She struck them hard enough to set the wooden rack rocking, and a bowl rolled off and cracked open on the hard ground. Kitty gave a yowl of horror as she saw shards of priceless pottery all over the floor.

And, just at that moment, a bolt scraped back noisily from the caravan door. Someone was coming out!

Chapter Seven

TRAPPED!

'Hide!' hissed Mr Dog. He snatched the bedraggled Flip-Flop from the water dish and carried her underneath the caravan, while Socks bounced over to join them with Shoe and Sneaker riding on his back.

As soon as Mr Dog disappeared from view

beneath the caravan, a woman's legs appeared

above, sticking out from below a dressing gown.

'Kitty! Oh, you naughty girl!' Kitty seemed

frozen with horror as the woman bustled over

and scooped up the black cat. 'I'm going to have

to put that bowl back together. No more playing

outside for you this morning. Come on . . .'

With a miaow of dismay, Kitty was whisked

back inside the caravan and the door slammed

shut behind her.

Mr Dog breathed a sigh of relief. 'It's meant to

be good luck when a black cat crosses your path.

But I think her *owner* was much luckier for us!'

'She was too busy looking at the broken bowl

to notice the tunnel by the fence,' Socks agreed.

Shoe nuzzled up to Flip-Flop. 'You were awesome, Sis!'

'You really were.' Sneaker kissed her nose. 'You showed that mean cat who was boss!'

'I'm so sorry I had to drop you like that, Flip-Flop, and give you your first bath.' Mr Dog bowed his head to her. 'Will you ever forgive me?'

'Yes.' Flip-Flop dried herself against Mr Dog's furry legs. 'But I don't think I like baths very much!'

'Mr Dog?' Shoe looked up at him, wide-eyed. 'Where's our mum?'

'Please can we find her now?' asked Sneaker, and Flip-Flop nodded.

'We will start searching at once.' Mr Dog edged cautiously from underneath the caravan, sniffing the air for a trace of rabbits. But he smelled humans instead – and froze as a man walked out from the Portakabin on the other side of the courtyard. It was the same man who had taken Mother Rabbit away in the trap. The caravan door creaked open overhead, and Mr Dog retreated under cover.

'What happened out here, Jo?' said the man. 'I was woken up, and—' He saw the broken bowl. 'Oh no . . .'

'Sorry, Hussan. My silly cat got carried away. Probably mousing again.'

'It would be quite a mouse that made *that*.' The man, Hussan, was pointing to the tunnel under the fence. 'What in the world . . . Did Misha's lurcher do this?'

'Can't have – she took him home with her last night.' Now Jo, a slim lady with short brown hair, was bending over the hole. 'From the way

the earth's fallen, I'd say something has pushed its way through rather than dug its way out.'

(*What a clever human*, thought Mr Dog approvingly.)

'It's too small for a person, so we can rule out thieves or vandals.' Hussan checked the racks. 'Nothing's been taken . . .?'

'No, I don't think so.' Jo paused. 'Do you think rabbits could've done this?'

'An army of intelligent rabbits, you mean?'
Hussan grinned. 'Wanting revenge on us for
taking so many of them away?'

'Don't!' Jo said. 'The ones we caught are
the lucky ones. I can't bear to think of the
exterminators coming next week to get rid of
the rest. They may be pests but it doesn't feel
right.'

(Sneaker, Shoe and Flip-Flop couldn't stifle
their gasps, and Socks was so shocked his ears
flew up in the air. Mr Dog snuggled against all
four of them.)

'At least we're saving *some* of the little rascals,'
said Hussan. 'They'll have a lovely new life in the

national park, safely away from the dig and the farmer's fields.'

'Nashy-null park,' Shoe echoed.

Flip-Flop's nose was quivering. 'Is that where Mum has gone?'

'Will we ever see her again?' asked Sneaker.

Mr Dog nodded firmly, although Socks looked less certain.

'It'll be a useful life for them there too,' Jo went on. 'That Park Authority is trying to preserve the grassland. Rabbits will eat the gorse and brambles, clearing the turf for low-growing plants. That will attract butterflies and insects, and encourage all kinds of birds to nest there—'

'I know, Jo, but we can't catch every single one by hand – or lurcher – and take them away, can we?' Hussan put a hand on her shoulder. 'It just isn't practical. We had no idea that this dig would prove to be so important – or so delicate. Rabbit habits have already made our job here a hundred times harder. If they're allowed to go on burrowing . . .'

'I know,' said Jo sadly. 'I just wish we could give all the rabbits a happier life in that park!'

'Perhaps we should put signs up,' Hussan joked. 'Rabbit Sanctuary, this way!' With some effort, he picked a heavy crate from beside the rack of relics and placed it over the hole. 'There.

That should keep out whatever got in.'

Socks squeaked softly in dismay. 'Oh no, now we're trapped!'

'What if whatever-got-in's still here somewhere?' Jo looked around worriedly. 'I'm going to keep Kitty safely locked up inside till we're sure.'

'That's good news, anyway,' whispered Mr Dog.

'Well, no need to wake the others yet.' Hussan yawned and stretched, as if he weren't quite awake himself. 'I'll have a look around, make sure nothing's been taken or damaged, just in case.'

'Splendid plan, my dear Hussan,' breathed Mr Dog as Jo clomped back inside her caravan. 'Now we can follow him for a guided tour of the dig!'

'Really?' Socks twitched his nose crossly (which only made him look more adorable). 'You want us to follow a known rabbit-catcher out in the open, with our only escape route blocked off?'

'I'm not suggesting we dance a conga with him!' Mr Dog protested. 'We need to find three things – firstly, poor Mother Rabbit. Secondly, a new way out of here. And thirdly, a way to save all the other rabbits before it's too late.' His eyes were shining even in the shadows. 'And while Hussan is looking for us, he won't expect us to be following close behind him, will he?'

'It sounds dangerous,' said Shoe.

Flip-Flop looked down at the ground. 'But we've got to risk it.'

'Mum would do anything for us and Socks,' Sneaker agreed. 'We're a family.'

'Er, yes. We are.' Socks quickly washed himself, so he didn't have to look at her. 'Of course we are.'

'Let's get going,' said Mr Dog. He knew the little bunnies were hungry and exhausted and couldn't last much longer. 'We must move as softly as dandelion clocks on a summer breeze . . . Come on!'

Still crawling, he led the way to the other side

of the caravan and poked his head out to check

the coast was clear. Nothing moved, except for

Hussan, who was heading across the dig site, so

he led Shoe, Socks, Flip-Flop and Sneaker out

into the sunlight.

Kitty glared at them from the grimy caravan window, her paws pressed up against the glass with longing. Mr Dog wagged his tail and padded lightly after Hussan, though his heart was feeling heavy. He badly wanted to make everything right around here.

But how?

Chapter Eight

THE SEARCH

Mr Dog led Socks, Shoe, Flip-Flop and Sneaker after Hussan in a crocodile. The archaeologist went first to a shed full of tools to check it hadn't been disturbed. Mr Dog and the others hid behind a dustbin while he did so.

Hussan's second place to visit was the snack van. He checked the shutters were still secure, pulled on the handle to open the door and looked inside. Mr Dog caught a wonderful whiff of sausages, one of his favourite foods. But under that he caught a very different smell wafting faintly on the breeze from across the site.

'Rabbits,' he breathed. 'Lots and lots of rabbits!' Working out the wind direction, he looked across the site, past a pair of big tents to a large rickety lean-to, built up against a section of the fence. A door with two bolts, top and bottom, secured the way in. *Come on, Hussan*, thought Mr Dog, *get checking over there.*

But Hussan did not go in the lean-to's direction. Instead, he made for one of the tents. Mr Dog and his group followed cautiously again, but the mutt called a stop when Hussan walked straight past the lean-to to check on another generator. With a sinking feeling he realised that Hussan was only checking up on things he thought were valuable to the site – and he had amply demonstrated that rabbits, in his view, were anything but! Besides, the bolts on the door would make it impossible for anyone but a human being to make their way inside. Hussan would never check on the lean-to!

'Change of plan,' Mr Dog muttered, leading

the way swiftly but stealthily towards the lean-to. 'Rabbits, I'm sure your mother is inside that shelter. We just need to find a way to get to her!'

The animals had a couple of close calls. Socks knocked over a broom that brought Hussan dangerously close to discovering them; Mr Dog just managed to herd his posse behind some paving slabs in time. They had barely moved to the shelter of a large tarpaulin, hanging from a washing line, when Jo, the other archaeologist, walked past. She had collected the shards of broken pottery in a small plastic basin and was ready to try to put the pieces back together.

Socks rose up to whisper in Mr Dog's ear.

'That lady reminds me of my owner!'

Except Jo actually seems to be fond *of rabbits,*
thought Mr Dog sadly. 'Wait here, bunnies,' he
whispered. 'I'm just going to scout out that
lean-to, to see if I can find a way in for us all.'

As he started away, Socks came after him. He glanced back, checking that Shoe, Flip-Flop and Sneaker couldn't hear.

'Mr Dog,' he said, nose twitching, 'you do think my owner is coming back for me . . . don't you?'

Mr Dog hesitated. 'No, Socks, I'm afraid I don't. And I think, deep down, you know that too.'

Socks gave a quiet, shivery sigh. 'They should've come back for me at once, shouldn't they?' He shook his head helplessly. 'Why would they take me out into the wild? What did I do to make them want to get rid of me? I let children pick me up. I never bit anyone . . .'

'It wasn't your fault.' Mr Dog gave him a supportive nudge with his nose. 'Sometimes people get pets with good intentions, but things change. Perhaps they had to move abroad, or to a house with no garden? Perhaps they couldn't afford to look after you any more? Or perhaps they decided that a pet was just too much of a tie?' He sighed. 'People can be silly and selfish. I'm sorry.'

'Thank you,' said Socks. He washed his whiskers and twitched his floppy ears. 'Well, anyway, Sneaker, Flip-Flop and Shoe deserve to be with their mother. Let's find her.'

'Yes, Socks, let's.' Mr Dog grinned. 'Come on.

You check one side of the lean-to and I'll check the other.'

The lean-to had recently been painted, and Mr Dog's nose was overwhelmed by the smell. The door was securely bolted so they couldn't get in that way. And though the shelter looked rough in places – the wooden walls nailed and braced together quite clumsily – it was strong enough to resist them breaking in.

Mr Dog doubled back to talk to Socks. 'Did you find any sneaky ways inside?'

'None,' Socks said sadly. 'How can we get to the rabbits locked up in there?'

'Hmmm.' Mr Dog looked at Socks. 'I've got

a plan, but it's risky. Whatever happens to me, you *must* get Shoe, Flip-Flop and Sneaker back to their mother. They can't last much longer.'

'Me?' Socks cringed. 'Alone?'

'You can do this. You have to.' He gave Socks a pointed look. 'They're family . . . remember?'

Socks drooped his ears. 'Yes. All right. You can rely on me.'

'I know,' Mr Dog said before smiling and nudging Socks towards the bunnies. Then he got up on his back legs and banged his front paws against the door of the lean-to, rattling it as hard as he could. The bolts held, but the noise was like a gun firing, and the rabbits inside gave a chorus of nervous squeaks.

Come on, Hussan, thought Mr Dog. *You've got to investigate this . . .*

Sure enough, Hussan soon appeared, poking his head out from one of the buildings. He hurried towards the lean-to, and Mr Dog quickly ran and hid behind it. *Good man,* he thought. *For all you know, whatever made that noise is inside . . .*

With relief, he heard the scrape of the bolts and the wooden door creak open. The squeaking of dozens of rabbits filled the air as Hussan went inside.

Squeak **SQUEAK** *Squeak* SQUEAK

SQUEAK **Squeak** SQUEAK

SQUEAK SQUEAK

Mr Dog reappeared from hiding and looked over to where Socks was waiting worriedly with Shoe, Flip-Flop and Sneaker. 'Good luck!' he whispered.

Then he turned back to the door and barked as loudly as he could.

Hussan immediately came outside again, frowning at the sight of Mr Dog. Mr Dog charged towards him and jumped up enthusiastically, pushing Hussan backwards before springing away to sit in the doorway, tongue hanging out, panting.

'What the . . . ?' said Hussan. 'It's you again. The stray dog from yesterday!'

Mr Dog woofed and ran away from the lean-to, hoping with all his heart that Hussan would not bolt the door before he followed. To make doubly sure, Mr Dog ran over to the snack van, stood on his hind legs and scrabbled at the door handle.

'Oh no you don't!' Hussan said warningly.

I'm rather afraid I do! thought Mr Dog as the door swung open and he dived inside. *He'll come after me all the more if I've got something he wants . . .* He used a combination of paws and jaws to force open the little fridge inside and quickly bit into a long string of sausages. *That'll do*, he thought. *Distracting and delicious!*

'Got you!' came a man's booming voice behind him. Hussan stood in the doorway with one of the big rabbit nets, ready to hurl it over Mr Dog . . .

Chapter Nine

RABBIT TREASURE

Desperately, Mr Dog lunged forward with the sausages. Then he darted through Hussan's legs before the net could entangle him. He ran out into the courtyard, galloping like a racehorse – heading straight for the crate Hussan had placed over the hole. At the last possible second, he veered away and

struck the crate with his shoulder. The jolt sent
pain searing through Mr Dog's side, but while the
impact was enough to shift the crate sideways a
little, it wasn't enough to uncover the hole.

'What on earth has he got in that box?' Mr Dog
groaned, snaffling one of the sausages for strength.
He saw that Hussan was coming for him again
with a face like thunder. This time Mr Dog darted
behind him and circled him, trailing the string of
sausages from his mouth. As Hussan tried to change
direction, his legs tangled in the sausage lasso and
he tumbled against the crate, knocking it over!

Mr Dog abandoned the sausages and hared away back to the lean-to, panting wildly, making for the still open door. He saw that the space inside was filled with large hutches one on top of another and each containing four or five rabbits. Socks had hopped up on to a bag of grain to reach a second-floor hutch, and Shoe, Flip-Flop and Sneaker were scrambling up to join him to get closer to . . .

Mother Rabbit!

Mr Dog's heart soared with happiness. There she was, pressed up against the bars of her hutch, while three other rabbits stuck inside with her watched on in puzzlement.

'My bunnies!' cried Mother Rabbit. 'All three of you!'

'And Socks!' said Shoe, jumping up and down.

'Yes, don't forget him!' squeaked Flip-Flop, and Sneaker nodded.

'Mr Dog!' Mother Rabbit's eyes lit up still further. 'Oh, thank you, thank you. You kept your word. You've brought us back together.'

'Very nearly.' Mr Dog could see there was no

way the bunnies could get into their mother's hutch. 'Allow me to finish the job!' He jumped nimbly on to the sack of grain and forced his head against the lid of the rabbit hutch, opening it a little way. 'Sneaker, Shoe, Flip-Flop – use me as a ladder and squeeze inside!'

'Yayyyyyyy,' squeaked the little bunnies, scampering up the scraggy mutt-mountain and then bundling through the open lid. All three landed safely in the thick sawdust beside their mother and within moments started to suckle contentedly.

'Just keep them out of sight as best you can,' Mr Dog advised her. 'You'll be all right – that goes for all you rabbits! You'll be taken to live safely in a national park. It's a fresh start – enjoy it.'

'Thank you,' said Mother Rabbit with a sweet and satisfied sigh.

Socks started to climb up Mr Dog, eager to squeeze into the hutch himself. But Mr Dog jumped down from the sack with Socks clinging to his back.

'Sorry, Socks.' Mr Dog lay down so the rabbit could hop off. 'The wild life is not the life for you.'

'But . . .' Socks jumped down, a quivering bundle of fur. 'But what will become of me, all alone?'

'I have one more idea,' Mr Dog told him. 'But we'll have to move fast!'

'Hussan!' Jo, Kitty's owner, was pointing to the lean-to. 'That dog – he's over here! Hussan?'

125

She hurried away to fetch him.

'Come on,' Mr Dog told Socks. 'One last mad rush. And be careful not to be seen. Not yet, anyway . . .'

Slipping away back to the cover of the hanging tarpaulin, Mr Dog and Socks watched as both Hussan and Jo entered the lean-to. Then they ran and hopped together back to the courtyard, where Hussan's unfortunate tumble had pushed the crate away from the hole.

'This is where we came in,' said Mr Dog, 'and it's where I'll go out.'

Socks squeaked. 'B-b-but what about me?'

Mr Dog didn't answer. He just dived into the

hole, wriggled back under the fence and into the field.

Socks gasped. Had he really been abandoned?

But, seconds later, Mr Dog returned with his mouth full. 'Here.' He opened his jaws and six of the old gold coins fell out, pinging over the muddy floor of the courtyard. 'You're going to buy your bed and board with this haul of ancient money!'

'What?' Socks stared. 'You're crazy!'

'*You're* rich,' Mr Dog retorted. 'Archaeologists love old coins – and Jo clearly loves animals too. If we put you both together, it'll cause quite a stir. How many rabbits are in the habit of finding coins? None! Except for you. People will want to know where you came from, who's looking after you . . .'

Socks's eyes widened. 'I might find my owner again!'

'Or you might find a brand-*new* owner,' Mr Dog suggested. 'One who'll look after you properly.'

Socks looked down at the coins and placed a paw on them. 'What a fantastic plan. Thank you, Mr Dog. You're brilliant!'

'*Quite* brilliant,' Mr Dog agreed cheerily. Then he heard footsteps hurrying from the direction of the lean-to; Hussan and Jo were coming to the courtyard. 'I'd better clear off,' he said, 'and leave you to your big moment.'

Socks smiled and nodded. 'But . . . what about all the other poor rabbits, out there? If the exterminator is coming for them . . .'

'I'll think of something, don't you worry.' Mr Dog backed up into the tunnel. 'I'm called Mr Dog, remember? The "Mister" is short for "He's Never *Missed a* Thing" . . . probably!'

With that, he wriggled away through the muddy tunnel and into the freedom of the field beyond, just as Hussan and Jo burst into view.

Socks, sitting amid the money, looked up at the humans innocently, twitching his nose in a most appealing fashion. 'Were you looking for something?' he squeaked.

They couldn't understand him, of course. But they could clearly see that the gold coins were very old and very rare and very valuable. Hussan fell to his knees in shock and started to gather them, while Jo picked up Socks.

'Well, you're a beautiful boy, aren't you?' she said. 'What a morning for mysteries! Where on earth did you come from with a treasure hoard like this?'

'Well, there was this dog, see . . .' Socks began.

Jo could never know what he was saying, but it was a story Socks intended to say out loud as often as possible – a story about a brave, scraggy mutt with a good heart and a marvellous mind, who ran headlong into adventure, helping others along the way.

Chapter Ten

NEW BEGINNINGS

A week later, one warm evening as the sun was setting, Socks sat in his spacious new two-storey hutch on the patio, looking out over rolling countryside. Two more rabbits – a mini Lop named Munchy and a Lilac called Ness – lay asleep in some hay beside him. Socks had been out in a run, munching sweet green grass all day, still marvelling at how his life had changed.

His name had changed too; since he'd been found with the old gold coins, Jo from the dig had called him 'Treasure'. The story of the 'bunny in the money' had got into the local news and he'd had all sorts of people sticking carrots and cameras in front of his face. Appeals were made to Socks's old owners, but no one had come forward.

Happily, Jo from the dig had felt that Munchy and Ness would enjoy some more company, and so she'd taken 'Treasure' home. Her garden was twice the size of his old place with views across the national park. As he gazed out, Socks – he would always think of himself as Socks, whatever others called him – wondered if Sneaker, Shoe, Flip-Flop and their mother had made it safely to freedom.

Suddenly, Socks froze. He'd heard a noise on the patio. A dark four-legged figure was watching him from across the concrete.

'Well, well,' came a familiar voice. 'So it is you! I knew you were around here somewhere, but thought my nose was playing tricks on me . . .'

'Mr Dog!' Socks bounced up and down in his cage. 'Mr Dog, it's so nice to see you. Look at my new house! Isn't it wonderful? I'm a celebrity, you know . . .'

'I *do* know,' Mr Dog agreed, ears lopsided, his spotted neckerchief ruffled. 'The lady I've been lodging with loves your story; she's been telling all her friends. I heard that you'd been rehomed somewhere with a view of the park, which is why I came looking. There's something I thought you'd like to see.'

'What's that?'

'Well, you getting in the news caused a lot of interest in rabbits.' Mr Dog licked his nose. 'And I think your new owner might have let slip to a journalist that the local wild rabbits were facing a short and unhappy future. There was a public outcry.'

'There was?' Socks's ears stood up. 'So the wild rabbits are safe now?'

'Well, since they weren't welcome on that private land, disturbing the dig and eating the farmer's crops, the local villages decided to work together.' Mr Dog looked very happy. 'There were no end of volunteers turning up to help catch the rabbits . . . and move them across to the national park.'

Socks boggled. 'ALL the rabbits?'

'Well, no. There were plenty they couldn't reach, and plenty more who didn't understand and stayed hidden in their burrows.' Mr Dog smiled. 'Which is why I thought I'd better get involved.'

Socks smiled back. 'Of course you did.'

'It was Hussan's idea, really – do you remember? He told Jo they should put up signposts for the wild bunnies, directing them to the national park. But humans don't speak rabbit, as I do. I scratched arrows into tree trunks and on stones: "*Rabbit Paradise – this way!*" and spread the word as best I could. "*All the grass you can eat – and* clover, *too.*"' Mr Dog sat on his haunches. 'I got every last rabbit so excited about that national park that . . . well, see for yourself.'

Socks peered past Mr Dog. All rabbits have good long-distance vision, and his was better than most. He realised that one of the rolling fields was alive with silver-grey movement – a wave of wild rabbits, hopping, jumping and tumbling through the hedgerows into the wide expanse of the parkland.

'They've come a long way,' said Mr Dog. 'And now they've reached their happy ending.'

'I can't believe it!' Socks shivered with delight. 'It's impossible.'

'Impossible things are usually possible things hiding behind a tree,' Mr Dog declared. 'Those rabbits will be safe now. Do give them a wave now and then, won't you? I expect that Shoe, Sneaker and Flip-Flop will be waving back at you.'

139

'Oh, I will. I will, I will, I will.' Socks hopped closer to the wire front of his hutch. 'Thank you, my friend. For everything.'

Mr Dog bowed politely. 'My dear Socks, I wouldn't have missed an adventure like this for all the world!'

'Where will you go now?'

'Well, I'm rather like that Roman dig we visited – I'm *roamin'* all over the place!' Mr Dog got up, his tail swishing merrily. 'I think perhaps I'll head for the coast. I do like to spend summer by the sea.' With a quiet woof of farewell, Mr Dog turned and trotted away.

'Happy travels,' said Socks. 'And good luck.'

'Good luck? Oh yes. Yes, indeed.' Mr Dog

looked back and gave the rabbit one last doggy

grin. 'I never travel without it!'

Notes from the Author

I love rabbits. I can still feel the warm trickle of tears as I read *Watership Down*. It was a book that had a huge influence on me and brought me close to an animal that I would usually only glimpse fleetingly as it tore across a field.

My first pet rabbit was, of course, named after another famous rabbit, Peter. He was a Netherland Dwarf and lived in a hutch with two guinea pigs for company. He had a beautiful white pelt that was so soft. And his ears. Those ears were incredible. I sobbed for a week when he died.

Having spent much of the last two decades working in the countryside, I have learned that to those farming the land, these small animals can, of course, be a pest but as with everything, we can both live in harmony. Rabbits provide a food source for birds of prey as well as keeping shrubs down and encouraging wildflower meadows.

Rabbits have an emotional draw over me. They have the power to take me back to my childhood. I hope this tale will help a new generation of young readers to connect with our countryside and the riches of its flora and fauna.

What should you do if you think a baby wild rabbit has been abandoned?

Young rabbits start to come out from the burrow at around eighteen days old when they will look like small adults. Never pick them up, unless they are injured.

If you are worried that a rabbit or hare could have been abandoned, you should keep a look-out from a safe distance. This may mean keeping watch overnight to see if the mother rabbit returns.

You shouldn't disturb a burrow as this could cause the mother to abandon her young. If a baby rabbit is found above ground with its eyes closed, it could mean that it's been dug out of its burrow by a predator. Only then would it need rescuing and taking for rehabilitation.

If you see a pet rabbit running free in a wild area, you should tell a grown-up as quickly as possible as it will need to be rescued. Do not approach it yourself as it may carry disease or parasites.

Join Mr Dog as he seeks out

his next adventure . . .

MR DOG
AND THE SEAL DEAL